D1270609

Praise for *The Clothesline Code*

"The story of *The Clothesline Code* is one of great fascination! Just as messages were sent by this ingenious method, this delightful book now sends out its messages of bravery and fortitude—an important chronicle of African American history. Written masterfully for young readers, it will capture the imagination of adults as well. It relates a little-known aspect of the uniquely American journey toward freedom, exemplified by two extraordinary individuals, Lucy Ann and Dabney Walker, Civil War spies and freedom seekers. A book to treasure and inspire future generations!"

—Norman Schools, longtime member of the Stafford County Historical Society and author of *Virginia Shade: An African American History of Falmouth, Virginia*

"This story offers a glimpse into a side of the war seldom explored—Black men and women who risked their lives as spies for the Union, just as other Black individuals had done for the American cause in the Revolutionary War. This story is educational, well-researched, and enjoyable reading."

—Kenneth A. Daigler, retired CIA officer and author of *Spies, Patriots, and Traitors: American Intelligence in the Revolutionary War* (Georgetown University Press: 2014) and *Black Dispatches* (CIA website)

"Lucy Ann and Dabney Walker are American heroes. Their covert operations at the heart of the Civil War in Virginia should inspire all of us to do what is right instead of easy, find our courage when surrounded by danger, and spring into action when the way forward becomes clear. *The Clothesline Code: The Story of Civil War Spies Lucy Ann and Dabney Walker* sends that message, loud and clear."

—Mary Belcher, historian, Walter Pierce Park Cemeteries Archaeology and Commemoration Project, Washington, D.C.

"A wonderful tribute that shares the inspirational story of the courage of Blacks who risked their lives for the freedom of others."

—Dawn Chitty, EdD, director of education at the African American Civil War Museum, Washington, D.C.

More praise for *The Clothesline Code*

"This true story of two formerly enslaved Black people who turned clothing into a weapon is enlightening and engaging. Halfmann's story informs readers of the bravery and sacrifice two people and an army took on to save a nation from the chains of slavery. The illustrations share emotion and draw the reader into the era."

—Kristi Bernard, blogger and book reviewer at Kristi's Book Nook
and Multicultural Children's Book Day

"Be prepared for page after page of surprises in this accurate and dramatically written and illustrated profile of Civil War heroes Lucy Ann and Dabney Walker. This is an impressive account of the brilliance, bravery, and boldness of a married couple who escaped enslavement to become spies for Union forces. They were praised while alive but have been overlooked by history—until NOW!"

—Sandy Brehl, retired elementary teacher and author of the middle grade
WWII historical trilogy *Odin's Promise*

"*The Clothesline Code* is a true story of the daring, danger, and devotion of the Walkers, a couple who escaped slavery and found a unique way to help the Union during the Civil War. Halfmann's vivid writing and Mason's emotive illustrations will engage both youth and adults."

—Jane Healy, library associate

"Vermont Avenue Baptist Church (aka Fifth Baptist Church) is honored and excited to share with others the legacy of Dabney and Lucy Ann Walker and their contributions more than 150 years ago. What a commitment in the face of life-threatening obstacles, and an example of using what was available! Readers are encouraged to read how the Union spies used laundry for one cause and Dabney later helped a Union wagon driver (co-founder and first pastor of this church) serve people in another cause."

—Vermont Avenue Baptist Church, Washington, D.C.

The Clothesline CODE

The Story of CIVIL WAR SPIES LUCY ANN and DABNEY WALKER

written by Janet Halfmann | illustrated by Trisha Mason

Brandylane Publishers, Inc.

ISBN: 978-1-951565-57-2
LCCN: 2020921338

Designed by Michael Hardison
Production managed by Mary-Peyton Crook

Printed in the United States of America

Published by
Brandylane Publishers, Inc.
5 S. 1st Street
Richmond, Virginia 23219

Brandylane
Publishers, Inc.
Publishing books since 1985

brandylanepublishers.com

For the thousands of Black people who helped the Union (in ways large and small, and often at great risk to themselves) win the Civil War, and for the crowds of protesters of all races marching today to demand changes to ensure that Black lives of today—and the future—truly do matter.

Author's Note

This story of Lucy Ann and Dabney Walker is true to the known facts of their lives and the society of their time. I had to imagine some scenes and thoughts, but they are based on documented events and actions.

Although many Union scouts wore civilian clothes, we have pictured Dabney in an army uniform. We did that because Union Captain George F. Noyes wrote in 1863 that Dabney "sallied forth with military cap, blue coat" as the usual guide for the cavalry.

Dabney Walker stared up the hill, captivated by the Union soldiers waving red-and-white flags. Two soldiers took turns holding a long flagpole and waving the flag to the right and left, over and over again, with dash and flourish.

Fifty-two-year-old Dabney had just been assigned to the camp's brand-new intelligence unit, and he wanted to know more about these flags. He asked the officer leading the flag drill to explain what the movements meant.

The officer told Dabney that the flag waving was a code meant for communicating across long distances on a battlefield. The code was simple, but it worked extremely well. A flag wave to the left stood for the number 1, a flag wave to the right stood for the number 2. Different combinations of these two numbers stood for each letter of the alphabet. Strung together, the letters spelled out messages.

To make things clearer, the officer offered to demonstrate the letter C. He called out 2-1-2, and a soldier trained as a flagman whipped the flag

to his right,

then his left,

then his right again, swiftly and precisely.

Excited, Dabney hurried off to locate his wife, Lucy Ann. He found her, as usual, under the clothesline, hard at work as a camp laundress. The couple and their teenage daughter, Sarah, had fled slavery and escaped to this Union camp in northeast Virginia about a year earlier. Since then, Dabney had worked as a cook and a valued scout for the camp, a Union stronghold in this otherwise slave state. As a native Virginian, Dabney was so skilled at finding the hiding places of the enemy Confederate army that they offered a $1,500 reward for his head!

Now in early 1863, the Union camp's new leader, Major General Joseph Hooker, wanted to know every detail about the Confederate army. He was especially interested in General Robert E. Lee's forces directly across the Rappahannock River from the Union camp.

Dabney was ready and determined to be the best spy ever. Learning how the flags sent messages gave him a big idea.

Dabney grabbed a pillowcase and put it on the end of a stick.

He waved it first to his right,

then to his left,

then to his right again,

explaining to Lucy Ann that the movements stood for the letter C. He told her he wanted to come up with their own signals. Then they could sneak into Confederate headquarters across the river and use the signals to send secrets back to the Union camp.

Lucy Ann was eager to help, but she wondered what they could use instead of letters—when they were enslaved, Dabney and Lucy Ann hadn't been allowed to learn to read and write. Plus, they needed something that was easy to see across the river but wouldn't attract unwanted attention.

The couple thought long and hard, all the while watching the laundry on the clothesline whipping in the wind. Then it hit them—they could use laundry on a clothesline to send signals across the river! For Lucy Ann, who had spent her entire life washing clothes for others, the idea made perfect sense.

But Dabney had second thoughts. If they used laundry to signal, Lucy Ann would have to be the one to go into enemy territory to steal and send Confederate secrets. If the enemy found out she was a spy, she would almost certainly be hanged.

But Lucy Ann had made up her mind, and that was it!

The couple had already faced grave dangers by escaping slavery. Both were willing to take more risks to help others gain freedom.

Creating the clothesline code was a huge job. The Confederate army was spread out in different units. Lucy Ann and Dabney had to create a unique laundry code to represent each unit.

The couple picked different colored shirts to stand for the forces of each Confederate leader: gray for Confederate General James Longstreet; white for General A.P. Hill; and red for General "Stonewall" Jackson.

Lucy Ann and Dabney plotted how they would move each general's shirt to show a movement of his forces. Removing the gray Longstreet shirt from the line would signal that his troops had moved nearer to Richmond, Virginia. Moving Hill's white shirt up the clothesline would mean his unit had moved upstream . . . and on and on.

A separate clothesline would signal what was happening at General Lee's headquarters across the river. A single item on the line would mean that Lee and his soldiers were on the move. Two pieces would signal no change. Three would warn that Lee was adding more troops to his forces.

The couple practiced the laundry movements again and again. Soon they both felt ready. Now they just needed a way to sneak Lucy Ann across the river.

In mid-February, an opportunity arose. Camp soldiers were helping a Confederate woman living in the Union-occupied area travel safely to visit friends across the river. Lucy Ann hid her face with her shawl and pretended to be the woman's servant. Lucy Ann's heart raced with fear that she would be stopped, but she forced herself to stay calm. The trick worked, and she was allowed on the boat.

Once on the opposite shore, Lucy Ann slipped away unseen toward Confederate headquarters. As she ran, she constantly looked all around to make sure no one saw her. Lucy Ann knew she faced harsh punishment, or even death, if she was caught. At General Lee's camp, she joined a group of enslaved workers doing laundry and acted as though she had been there all along. Soon she was washing clothes and cooking for General Lee and his officers. She and Dabney were

Before long, Dabney was providing vital information to Union officers about the enemy's movements—sometimes even before they happened. The officers puzzled over how he was getting such timely and accurate intelligence.

For a long time, Dabney kept the clothesline code a secret from other soldiers to keep Lucy Ann safe. Finally, after much pleading from the camp's officers, he took one of them to a high point with a clear view across the river. Dabney pointed and asked the officer if he could see a cabin with a clothesline.

The officer looked through his field glasses and nodded.

"Well," said Dabney, "that clothesline tells me in half an hour just what goes on at Lee's headquarters."

Dabney explained that his wife worked at the Confederate headquarters and secretly listened closely to everything being said there. The body servants of Confederate officers also shared secrets with her.

When Lucy Ann had information, she headed to the clothesline. She was careful not to rush or attract attention that might endanger her or her chance to spy. She kept clothes on the line at all times so as not to arouse suspicion.

The clothesline code could even handle tricky situations. One morning, Dabney reported lots of movement by the Confederate army. "But . . ." he said, "they're just making believe."

Surprised, an officer asked Dabney how he knew the enemy was playing a trick.

Dabney pointed to Lucy Ann's clothesline, at the two blankets pinned together.

He explained this was Lucy Ann's signal for troops being moved just to confuse the Union. "Why, that's her way of making a fish-trap; and when she pins the clothes together that way, it means that Lee is only trying to draw us into his fish-trap."

Then one day, the laundry fell silent. Not a single piece moved for days.

Had something happened to scare Lucy Ann? Had she been found out or put in jail?

Dabney's heart throbbed with dread that his wife was in danger. He couldn't eat or sleep. He feared she might have been hanged!

For several long days, he watched and worried, his heart aching and his fears growing. But still no clothes moved.

Finally . . . the laundry signaled again! What a relief! Dabney jumped up and down, punching the air with joy that Lucy Ann was all right.

Day after day until late April, Lucy Ann made the laundry whisper its secrets—and Dabney and the Union officers paid close attention.

With the onset of spring and good weather, it was time for General Hooker to lead his troops into battle. General Hooker had a bold plan to take the Confederate forces by surprise.

Thanks to the Walkers, the Union army was ready. General Hooker's spy unit had given him a clearer picture of the enemy than at any time since the war began. For that, he owed thanks to many—including the brave and dedicated Walkers. An officer praised the couple as being among the "promptest and most reliable" of General Hooker's spies. Lucy Ann and Dabney took tremendous risks to their lives in order to help others on the long journey toward freedom.

Afterword

From 1861 to 1865, the northern and southern states of the United States fought a civil war, primarily over slavery. Southerners wanted slavery to be legal in the nation's new territories, and northerners did not. The bitter division caused eleven southern slave states, including Virginia where the Walkers lived, to leave the United States and form the Confederate States of America. The northern states remained the United States of America, or the Union.

In the spring of 1863, despite General Hooker being extremely well informed about the enemy (thanks to the Walkers and other Union spies), the Union lost the battle now known as the Battle of Chancellorsville.

After the defeat, the Union troops again settled for several weeks on the northern bank of the Rappahannock River. Thankfully, Lucy Ann somehow managed to escape back to the safety of Union lines. No record exists of why her laundry signals had stopped for a time.

When the Union army left Virginia in June 1863 for battle elsewhere, the Walkers headed to Washington, D.C., their part-time home since September of 1862. They lived in Washington when they weren't needed by the Union army. While in D.C., Dabney helped create military maps in the city with Union Captain William H. Paine during November and December of 1862.

In May of 1864, Dabney again returned to Virginia to scout for the Union army during its drive toward Richmond. It is unknown whether Lucy Ann went with him or stayed in Washington.

Following the war, the Walkers continued to live in Washington, D.C. Dabney worked as a carpenter and laborer, and Lucy Ann as a laundress.

Along with six other formerly enslaved men, Dabney founded the Fifth Baptist Church (now Vermont Avenue Baptist) in Washington, D.C., on June 5, 1866.

The church was the scene of Sarah Walker's marriage in 1871 to Charles Barnes of Maryland. The couple had two children.

Unfortunately, little is known of the Walker family's life in Washington. Lucy Ann died at age sixty-six on June 12, 1880. Dabney remarried Rosa "Rosey" Dean in 1881. He died at age seventy-four on April 23, 1885.

Lucy Ann, Dabney, and their daughter and grandchildren are buried at Mt. Pleasant Plains Cemetery, Walter Pierce Park, in Washington, D.C.

Acknowledgements

I wish to especially thank military historian Albert Z. Conner, Jr. (now deceased) for providing me an article he wrote about the Walkers for the Moncure Conway Foundation of Stafford, Virginia. I also owe deep gratitude to my son, Drew Halfmann, for scouring the Civil War diaries of Captain William H. Paine at the New York Historical Society. Since Dabney assisted Captain Paine in mapmaking and surveying, I hoped Paine's diaries might mention the Walkers' clothesline signaling system, and they did just that—adding additional credibility to this amazing spying feat, for which official records are scarce. Thanks also to my editor Mary-Peyton Crook and illustrator Trisha Mason for helping me bring this important true story to life.

-Janet Halfmann

About the Author

Janet Halfmann is a multi-award-winning children's author who strives to make her books come alive for young readers and listeners. Many of her picture books are about animals and nature. She also writes picture book biographies about little-known people of achievement. Janet has written more than forty fiction and nonfiction books for children.

Before becoming a children's author, Janet was a daily newspaper reporter, children's magazine managing editor, and a creator of coloring and activity books for Golden Books. She is the mother of four and the grandmother of six. When Janet isn't writing, she enjoys gardening, exploring nature, visiting living-history museums, and spending time with her family. She grew up on a farm in Michigan and now lives in South Milwaukee, WI. You can find out more about Janet and her books on her website www.janethalfmannauthor.com.

About the Illustrator

Trisha Mason attended the Herron School of Art + Design (IUPUI), where she graduated with honors and a BFA in drawing and illustration. She has illustrated the children's book *Be Brave, Be Brave, Be Brave* by F. Anthony Falcon and has art featured in the book *She Votes* by Bridget Quinn. Mason currently resides in Plainfield, IN, where she enjoys creating watercolor pet portraits and taking walks with her fiancé, Jack, and her dog, Gilly. You can view more of Trisha's work on her website www.trishamasonart.com or her Instagram @trishabmason.

Reference for Quotes

All Dabney Walker and Union officer quotes about the operation of the clothesline code:

Moore, Frank, ed. *Anecdotes, Poetry, and Incidents of the War: North and South, 1860-1865.* "The Clothes-line Telegraph," New York: 1866, 263-264.

Selected References

Conner, Albert Z., Jr. "Dabney Walker and Family of Spotsylvania County," Moncure Conway Foundation, Stafford, VA.

"'Dabney,' the Colored Scout," from *Frank Moore's Anecdotes, Bangor Daily Whig & Courier* (Bangor, ME), December 6, 1866.

"Dabney, the Negro Scout of the Rappahannock," *The Liberator* (Boston, MA), August 8, 1862.

"Dabney Walker," *Index to the Reports of Committees of the House of Representatives for the First and Second Sessions of the Forty-Fifth Congress, 1877-'78,* Volume 1, Report No. 218, Washington: Government Printing Office, 1878.

"Famous War Scout Dies at His Home on East Fourth Street," *The Daily Argus* (Mount Vernon, NY), November 20, 1908.

Fishel, Edwin C. *The Secret War for the Union.* New York: Houghton Mifflin, 1996.

Letters Received by the Adjutant General, 1861-1870, Fold3 by Ancestry. Search for Dabney Walker.

Moore, Frank, ed. *Anecdotes, Poetry, and Incidents of the War: North and South, 1860-1865.* "The Clothes-line Telegraph," New York: 1866, 263-264.

Noyes, George Freeman (Captain, US Volunteers). *The Bivouac and the Battlefield.* New York: Harper & Brothers, 1863, 46-47.

"Paine the Pathfinder: The Notable Career of a Brooklyn Engineer," *Brooklyn Daily Eagle* (Brooklyn, NY), January 4, 1891.

Paine, William H. Diary, September 1862-June 1863. William H. Paine Papers, New York Historical Society.

Schools, Norman. *Virginia Shade: An African American History of Falmouth, Virginia.* Bloomington, IN: iUniverse, 2012.

"The Walter Pierce Park Cemeteries: Commemorating the African American and Quaker Cemeteries at Walter Pierce Park, Washington, DC": http://walterpierceparkcemeteries.org/

"What Contrabands Are Good For," *The Liberator* (Boston, MA), June 20, 1862.

CPSIA information can be obtained
at www.ICGtesting.com
Printed in the USA
BVHW021704150321
602576BV00010B/55